THE DEPUTATION

by

The Rev. W. Awdry

with illustrations by
John T. Kenney

GROLIER

Break Van

THE Fat Controller scolded both engines severely.

"There must be no more tricks," he said. "I shall be watching you both. I have to decide which of you is to stay." He strode away.

The twins looked glum. Neither wanted to stay without the other. They said so.

"Then what is tae dae?" wondered Douglas.

"Och!" said Donald. "Each maun be aye guid as ither. Syne he'll hae tae keep uz baith."

Their plan was good; but they had reckoned without a spiteful Brakevan.

The van had taken a dislike to Douglas. Things always went wrong when he had to take it out. Then his trains were late, and he was blamed. Douglas began to worry.

"Ye're a muckle nuisance," said Donald one day. "It's tae leave ye behind I'd be wantin'."

"You can't," said the van, "I'm essential."

"Och are ye?" Donald burst out. "Ye're naethin' but a screechin' an' a noise when a's said an' done. Spite Douggie wad ye? Tak that."

"Oh! Oh! Oh!" cried the van.

"Haud yer wheesht," said Donald severely. "There's mair comin' syne ye misbehave."

The van behaved better after that. Douglas's trains were punctual, and the twins felt happier.

Then Donald had an accident. He backed into a siding. The rails were slippery. He couldn't stop in time, and crashed through the buffers into a signalbox.

One moment the Signalman was standing on the stairs; the next, he was sitting on the coal in Donald's tender. He was most annoyed.

"You clumsy great engine," he stormed, "now you must stay there. You've jammed my points. It serves you right for spoiling my nice new Signalbox."

The Fat Controller was cross too. "I am disappointed, Donald," he said. "I did not expect such—er—clumsiness from you. I had decided to send Douglas back and keep you."

"I'm sorry, Sirr," but Donald didn't say what he was sorry for. We know, don't we?

"I should think so too," went on the Fat Controller indignantly. "You have upset my Arrangements. It is Most Inconvenient. Now James will have to help with the goods work, while you have your tender mended. James won't like that."

The Fat Controller was right. James grumbled dreadfully.

"Ony wan wad think," said Douglas, " that Donal had his accident on purrpose. I heard tell," he went on, "aboot an engine an' some tar wagons."

Gordon and Henry chuckled.

"Shut up!" said James. "It's not funny."

"Weel, weel, weel!" said Douglas innocently. "Shairly Jeames it wasna you? Ye dinna say!"

James didn't say. He was sulky next morning, and wouldn't steam properly. When at last he did start, he bumped the trucks hard.

"He's cross," sniggered the spiteful Brakevan. "We'll try to make him crosser still!"

"Hold back!" whispered the van to the trucks.

"Hold back!" giggled the trucks to each other.

James did his best, but he was exhausted when they reached Edward's station. Luckily Douglas was there.

"Help me up the hill please," panted James. "These trucks are playing tricks."

"We'll show them, said Douglas grimly.

"ComeonComeonCOMEON," puffed James crossly.

"Get MOV-in' you! Get MOV-in' you!" puffed Douglas from behind.

Slowly but surely the snorting engines forced the unwilling trucks up the hill.

But James was losing steam. "I can't do it. I can't do it," he panted.

"LAE IT TAE ME! LAE IT TAE ME!" shouted Douglas. He pushed and he puffed so furiously that sparks leapt from his funnel.

"Ooer!" groaned the van. "I wish I'd never thought of this." It was squeezed between Douglas and the trucks. "Go on! Go on!" it screamed; but they took no notice.

The Guard was anxious. "Go steady!" he yelled to Douglas. "The van's breaking."

It was too late. The Guard jumped as the van collapsed. He landed safely on the side of the line.

"I might have known it would be Douglas!"

"I'm sorry Sirr. Mebbe I was clumsy, but I *wadna* be beaten by yon tricksie van."

"I see," said the Fat Controller.

Edward brought workmen to clear the mess.

"Douglas was grand Sir," he said. "James had no steam left, but Douglas worked hard enough for three. I heard him from my yard."

"Two would have been enough," said the Fat Controller drily. "I want to be fair, Douglas," he went on. "I admire your determination, but . . . I don't know, I really don't know."

He turned and walked thoughtfully away.

The Deputation

"HE'LL send uz awa' for shair, Donal."

"I'm thinkin' ye're richt there, Douggie. The luck's aye been agin uz. An Engine disna ken what tae dae for the best."

Snow came early that year. It was heavier than usual. It stayed too, and choked the lines. Most engines hate snow. Donald and Douglas were used to it. They knew what to do. Their Drivers spoke to the Inspector, and they were soon coupled back to back, with a van between their tenders. Then, each with a snowplough on their fronts, they set to work.

They puffed busily backwards and forwards

patrolling the line. Generally the snow slipped away easily, but sometimes they found deeper drifts. Then they would charge them again and again, snorting, slipping, puffing, panting, till they had forced their way through.

Presently they came to a drift which was larger than most. They charged it, and were backing for another try. There was a feeble whistle, people waved and shouted.

"Losh sakes, Donal, it's Henry! Dinna fash yersel, Henry. Bide a wee. We'll hae ye oot!"

The Fat Controller was returning soon. The twins were glum. "He'll send uz back for shair," they said. "It's a shame!" sympathised Percy.

"A lot of nonsense about a signalbox," grumbled Gordon. "Too many of those, if you ask me."

"That Brakevan too," put in James. "Good riddance. That's what I say."

"They were splendid in the snow," added Henry. "It isn't fair." They all agreed that Something Must Be Done, but none knew what.

One day Percy talked to Edward about it.

"What you need," said Edward, " is a Deputation." He explained what that was.

Percy ran back quickly. "Edward says we need a Depotstation," he told the others.

"Of course," said Gordon, "the question is . . ."

". . . what is a desperation?" asked Henry.

"It's when engines tell the Fat Controller something's wrong, and ask him to put it right."

"Did you say *tell* the Fat Controller?" asked Duck thoughtfully. There was a long silence. "I propose," said Gordon at last, "that Percy be our—er—hum—disputation."

"HI!" squeaked Percy. "I can't."

"Rubbish Percy," said Henry. "It's easy."

"That's settled then," said Gordon.

Poor Percy wished it wasn't!

"Hullo Percy! It's nice to be back."

Percy jumped. Some trucks went flying.

"Er y-y-yes Sir, please Sir."

"You look nervous, Percy. What's the matter?"

"Please Sir, they've made me a Desperation Sir. To Speak to You Sir. I don't like it Sir."

The Fat Controller pondered. "Do you mean a Deputation, Percy?" he asked.

"Yes Sir, please Sir. It's Donald and Douglas Sir, they'll be turned into Scrap, Sir. That'd be dreadful, Sir. Please Sir, don't send them away, Sir. They're nice engines, Sir."

"Thank you, Percy. That will do." He walked away.

"I had a—er—deputation yesterday," said the Fat Controller. "I understand your feelings but I do *not* approve of interference." He paused impressively. "Donald and Douglas, I hear that your work in the snow was good. What colour paint would you like?" The twins were surprised. "Blue, Sirr, please."

"Very well. But your names will be painted on you. We'll have no more 'mistakes'."

"Thankye Sir. Dis this mean that the baith o' uz . . . ?"

The Fat Controller smiled. "It means . . ."

But the rest of his speech was drowned in a delighted chorus of cheers and whistles.

This book club edition published by Grolier 1995

Published by arrangement with Reed Children's Books
First published in Great Britain 1960 as part of *The Railway Series* No. 15
Copyright © William Heinemann Ltd. 1960
This edition copyright © William Heinemann Ltd. 1995